ADVENTURE STORY BOOK

Cry Wolf

Martian Invasion

Day of Disaster

The Cham-Cham

Sally Byford

CARLTON
BOOKS

CRY WOLF

Scott to the Rescue!

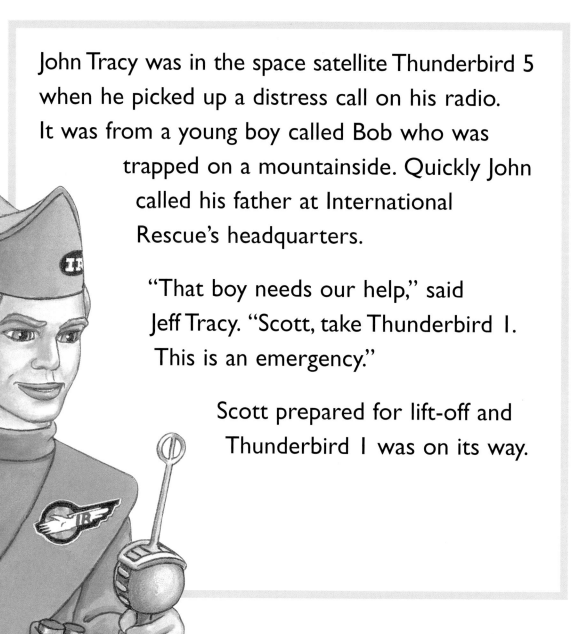

John Tracy was in the space satellite Thunderbird 5
when he picked up a distress call on his radio.
It was from a young boy called Bob who was
trapped on a mountainside. Quickly John
called his father at International
Rescue's headquarters.

"That boy needs our help," said
Jeff Tracy. "Scott, take Thunderbird 1.
This is an emergency."

Scott prepared for lift-off and
Thunderbird 1 was on its way.

Scott soon reached the mountain and ran to help. But Bob was not really in trouble. He had already been rescued – by another boy.

Bob and Tony Williams were just playing at International Rescue. They were very surprised when they saw the real Scott Tracy.

"You mustn't use your walkie-talkies again," said Scott. "International Rescue could miss a real emergency."

Bob and Tony were very sorry. They took Scott to their house at Charity Springs to meet their father.

"It won't happen again," said Mr Williams when Scott told him about the false alarm.

Mr Williams was worried. He ran a space station which took top-secret photographs. If the boys' story got into the newspapers, his enemies might find out where he lived.

But the false alarm was reported in the papers the very next day. In his temple, the Hood laughed to himself. He knew that Mr Williams took top-secret photographs and now he knew where to find him.

A few days later, the Hood was watching the house at Charity Springs from a distance. Bob and Tony came out. They were playing at their favourite game of International Rescue again and it was Tony's turn to hide. The Hood heard Tony say he was going to the old mines.

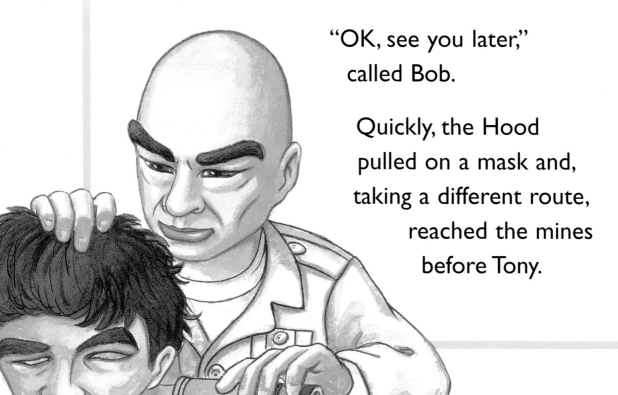

"OK, see you later," called Bob.

Quickly, the Hood pulled on a mask and, taking a different route, reached the mines before Tony.

When Tony and the Hood met at the mines, the Hood seemed friendly so Tony told him about the game.

"There's a good place to hide," said the Hood, pointing to a mine entrance.

Tony crept in through the narrow opening. Then, when Bob arrived, the Hood showed him Tony's hiding place. But as soon as Bob had gone in, the Hood blew up the mine. Rocks fell and covered the entrance.

The boys were trapped.

Bob and Tony were terrified. They knew they shouldn't use their walkie-talkies but they had to call for help. It was their only chance.

John was surprised to get another distress call from the boys. "We're trapped down a mine," said Bob. "It's not a game this time. Please believe us."

John called his father, but Jeff didn't believe the story. "They're just playing," he said. "It's another false alarm."

Meanwhile, the Hood had broken in at Charity Springs and was burning his way through the high-security darkroom walls.

Mr Williams, who was inside, was alarmed when he heard the noise. He quickly contacted Colonel Jameson, his commander. "It must be the Hood after the top-secret photographs," he said.

"We'll send help straight away," replied Colonel Jameson. "If he breaks through, destroy the photographs before he gets them."

Colonel Jameson called International Rescue and asked for help.

"So Bob and Tony weren't playing after all," said Jeff. "That man must have wanted the boys out of the way so he could steal the photographs."

Jeff gave the orders for immediate action. Scott took Thunderbird 1 to save Mr Williams, and Virgil and Alan took Thunderbird 2 to the mines.

"Quick," said Jeff. "Those boys are in great danger."

Back at Charity Springs, the Hood had burnt through the wall of the darkroom. He burst in and with his magic made Mr Williams go to sleep. Then he grabbed the photographs and made his escape.

Scott arrived just in time to see the Hood driving away from the house with the photographs. He jumped on to his hoverjet and sped off after him.

The Hood drove faster and faster along the steep mountain roads. Suddenly he lost control. The Jeep swerved dangerously round a corner, hurtled over the edge and exploded at the bottom.

"That's the last we'll see of him," said Scott as he rescued the photographs.

Scott didn't know that the Hood was still alive. He'd fallen from the Jeep and was caught in the branches of a tree. International Rescue had won this time but the Hood would soon be back with another evil plan.

Meanwhile, Virgil and Alan had found the boys almost buried under rubble and worked quickly to free them. They managed to drag them to safety just before the roof collapsed.

Mr Williams was overjoyed to have Bob and Tony back. "You saved the photographs from falling into the wrong hands, but more than that you saved my boys' lives," he said. "Thank you, International Rescue!"

MARTIAN INVASION

Virgil Defeats the Hood

The Hood had a plan to uncover International Rescue's secrets. He travelled to the desert in disguise to work on a film called *Martian Invasion*.

In the film the Martians had to bomb a cave where two police officers were hiding. The Hood planned to cause a terrible accident so that International Rescue would have to be called out.

Then he'd film them in action and sell their secrets to the mysterious General X.

First, the Hood needed help from his half-brother, Kyrano, who worked for International Rescue. In his temple, he used magic to get Kyrano in his power.

"Go to Thunderbird 1," the Hood ordered Kyrano, "and switch off the automatic camera detector."

So, while Kyrano was under the Hood's spell, he crept over to Thunderbird 1 and switched off the detector. Now the Hood would be able to film the aircraft without Scott knowing.

When the filming started, the two actors playing police officers hid in a cave and the Martians bombed them. Everyone was shocked by the size of the explosion. They did not know that the Hood had been at work. The cave started to collapse and water poured in.

"We'd better call International Rescue," said the Hood.

Mr Goldheimer, the director, called for help. "Two of the actors are trapped," he told Jeff Tracy. "Please come quickly!"

Scott and Virgil soon arrived in Thunderbirds 1 and 2. As soon as they saw what had happened, Virgil released the Excavator and started drilling through the rocks that blocked the cave's entrance.

Meanwhile the Hood was secretly filming every detail of International Rescue's equipment.

"My plan is working perfectly," he laughed.

Inside the cave, the two actors playing the police officers were very scared. They clung to the rocks, but the water was rising fast. Suddenly they heard Scott's voice on the radio.

"Stay calm," he said. "When I give the word, jump into the water. The pressure will carry you out through the hole we have drilled in the side of the mountain. Now, jump!"

The men jumped. They knew it was their only chance.

The two actors shot out of the hole just before the cave roof collapsed. They were wet and shivering, but they were safe. The rescue had been a success.

Scott was about to leave in Thunderbird 1 when Mr Goldheimer rushed up and took a photograph of him.

The camera detector didn't sound its alarm. Scott was puzzled.

"It must be switched off," he said. "Someone could have taken a film of the whole rescue."

Suddenly, they heard a Jeep speeding away.
Mr Goldheimer looked through his binoculars. It
was the Hood, without his disguise.

"That man's stolen a reel of film," he cried.

Scott knew it could be a film of the rescue.
He chased after the Hood in Thunderbird 1, but
the Jeep vanished into a tunnel.

The Hood called General X.

"I'll deliver the film as soon as I
have escaped from International
Rescue," he said.

Scott stopped outside the tunnel and contacted his father.

"There are two entrances to that tunnel, Scott," said Jeff. "I'll send Virgil in Thunderbird 2 to take your place. You must go to the other entrance."

"I'm on my way, father," said Scott.

"Don't let that film get away," said Jeff. "If our secrets are discovered, it will be the end of International Rescue."

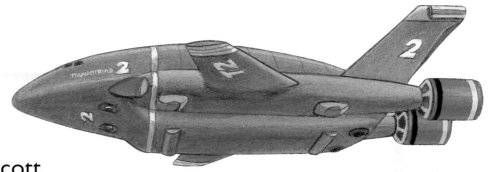

As soon as Scott had left to find the other entrance, the Hood made his escape. Virgil arrived just in time to see him driving away at top speed. Quickly, he contacted his father.

"Do everything you can to stop him, Virgil," said Jeff. "We've got to get that film."

Virgil bombed the mountains at the side of the road. There was a landslide and the Hood's Jeep was trapped.

The Hood jumped out of his Jeep and ran off. He hadn't gone far when he saw an empty plane. "Perfect!" he said, and he climbed in and took off.

He called General X on his radio to tell him that he had managed to escape from International Rescue and would soon be handing over the film. But then he realized that there was something wrong with the plane. It was dropping towards the ground because the controls were not working properly.

Scott was following close behind.

At last the Hood saw General X's villa ahead, but by now he couldn't control the plane at all. Scott watched as it crashed into the front of the villa. This was the end of the Hood's evil plan.

Scott contacted his father. "The film couldn't have survived that smash," he said.

"Well done," said Jeff. "Thanks to you and Virgil the Hood has been beaten and International Rescue's secrets are safe. This mission is now complete."

DAY OF DISASTER

Gordon Saves the Day!

There was great excitement when a space rocket had to be transported across the Allington Suspension Bridge. But it was only half-way over when disaster struck.

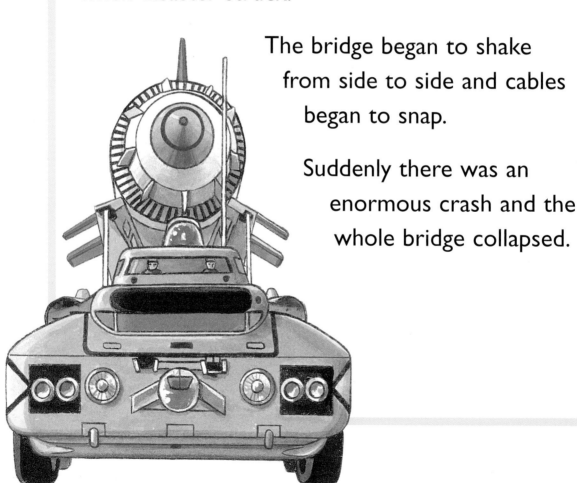

The bridge began to shake from side to side and cables began to snap.

Suddenly there was an enormous crash and the whole bridge collapsed.

The rocket plunged into the river. Then the automatic launch countdown started. In twelve hours, the rocket would blast off and be blown to pieces, with two men trapped inside the nose cone.

It took the Bridge Controller three hours to establish a radio link with the men. Inside the rocket, Frank and Bill were glad to hear his voice. "Have you called International Rescue?" asked Frank.

"We don't need them," said the Controller. "We have three floating cranes ready to pull you out."

Lady Penelope and Brains had watched the disaster on television and wanted to help. Parker drove them towards the bridge, but they were stopped by a policeman.

"I've got to get to those trapped men," said Brains.

"I'm afraid the way is completely blocked," said the policeman.

"Why don't you cut across the fields and make your own way to the bridge, Brains?" said Lady Penelope.

Brains walked to the bridge and managed to get into the control room. "Your equipment looks too old for a job like this," he said. "You'd better call International Rescue."

The Controller was very cross. "Watch this troublemaker," he told his assistant. "Don't let him near the bridge."

Brains quietly contacted John Tracy on his watch radio. "I've got a job for you," he said.

John contacted his father on the two-way TV.

"I've just heard from Brains. He says the equipment at Allington Bridge is very old. And there are only seven hours left before the rocket blasts off. They need our help."

"OK, John," said Jeff. "Tell Brains we'll be there as soon as we can. Scott, take Thunderbird 1 and check out what's happening. Gordon and Virgil, take Thunderbirds 2 and 4. Good luck, boys."

Inside the rocket, Frank and Bill watched the clock. There were five hours left when the Controller called again.

"We're ready," he said.

The huge cranes struggled to pull the rocket out, but it wouldn't move. One by one, the cranes sank into the river. The Controller's plan had failed.

"Only International Rescue can save us now," he said.

"They're already on their way," said Brains.

It wasn't long before Scott reached the bridge. "It looks pretty bad, father," he said. "I can't do anything until Virgil and Gordon arrive."

Thunderbird 2 got there an hour later. Virgil quickly dropped the pod into the water and released Gordon in Thunderbird 4.

Gordon investigated under water. He saw that the rocket was completely surrounded by rubble from the broken bridge. "It's a real mess down here," he told Brains.

Brains asked Virgil to clear the rubble away from the rocket using Thunderbird 2's giant grabs. Virgil worked as quickly as he could, but he didn't have much time left.

Inside the rocket, Frank and Bill had no idea what was happening.

"There are only fifteen minutes left," said Frank. "They can't help us now."

Brains contacted Gordon again. "Is the nose cone clear yet?" he asked.

"No, it's not," said Gordon. "We'll never make it in time."

Brains thought hard. "Try using the missiles," he said.

So Gordon fired at the rubble. Inside, Frank and Bill heard the explosions.

"They're trying to blow us to pieces," said Frank.

"We're going to be blown up anyway," said Bill. "Look at the time!" There were only eight minutes left.

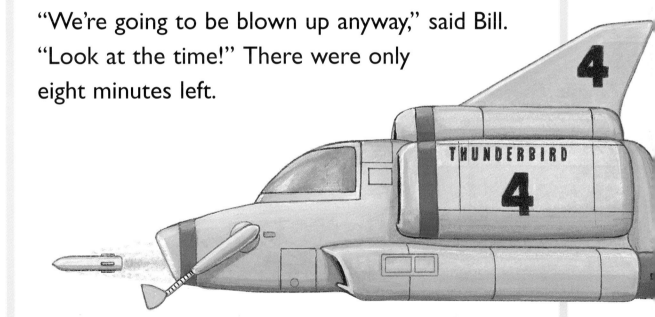

The missiles cleared the rubble. Then Gordon drove Thunderbird 4 into the nose cone at top speed. The cone broke free from the rest of the rocket and floated to the top of the river.

There were now five minutes to lift-off. Virgil lowered the claw from Thunderbird 2 and held the nose cone tightly. He lifted it out of the water and carried it to dry land.

Frank and Bill couldn't believe their luck. "We're out of the river," cried Bill. "And there's still half a minute to go!"

Seconds later, the countdown was over. The rocket blasted up into the sky. As everyone watched, it slowed down, started to fall and then exploded in a ball of flames.

"International Rescue has done it!" said the Controller.

Brains danced around the room feeling very happy.

It was the end of a disastrous day for Allington Suspension Bridge, but thanks to International Rescue Frank and Bill were safe at last.

THE CHAM-CHAM

Penelope the Pop Star!

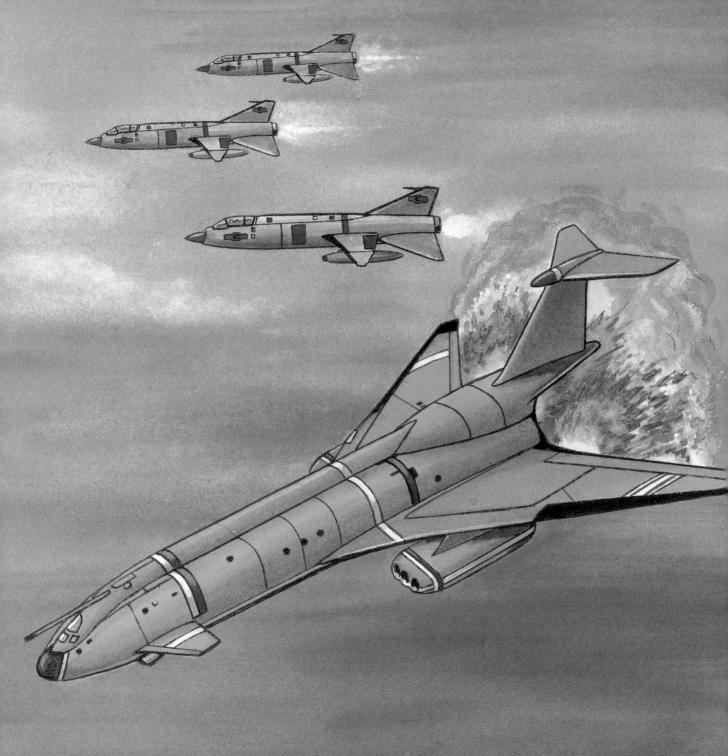

The air force had a very special job to deliver top-secret goods for the government. But each time they tried, their rocket transporters were bombed to the ground by enemy aircraft.

There was something very strange about the bombings.

Just before the attacks, the transporter pilots were always listening to the radio, to a song called "Dangerous Game" by the Cass Carnaby Five.

Alan Tracy wondered if someone was using the song to send a message to the enemy aircraft. "It could be their orders to attack," he said.

"Let's investigate," said Jeff.

Brains studied the song in his laboratory. "There's definitely some sort of message there," he said.

Lady Penelope was having tea when Jeff contacted her. "I want you and Tin-Tin to investigate the Cass Carnaby Five," he said. "They're playing at Paradise Peaks Hotel."

Lady Penelope and Tin-Tin travelled to the Paradise Peaks Hotel, high in the mountains. Lady Penelope disguised herself as a singer. Parker went on his own to the hotel. He found a job with Benino, the head waiter. The investigation had begun.

The Cass Carnaby Five were playing in the ballroom. Lady Penelope and Tin-Tin watched them closely.

"I can't believe they'd have anything to do with the bombings," said Tin-Tin.

After the show, Tin-Tin went to meet Cass Carnaby and his manager, Mr Olsen.

"'Dangerous Game' is my favourite song," said Tin-Tin. "But don't you get tired of playing the same tune all the time?"

Mr Olsen looked at her angrily and quickly left the room.

"The song isn't always the same," said Cass. "Sometimes Mr Olsen changes the music just before we play."

Tin-Tin decided to find out more about Mr Olsen.

Next morning, Lady Penelope and Tin-Tin went on their skis to Mr Olsen's house and watched him secretly through the window. He was working on a strange computer.

Tin-Tin used a zoom lens to get a closer look. On the screen, she saw the words: NEXT ROCKET TRANSPORTER DEPARTURE TODAY 14.00 HOURS. IT MUST BE DESTROYED.

"It's an order to bomb the transporter this afternoon," said Tin-Tin. "Let's get back to the hotel. We've got to warn Jeff!"

Mr Olsen saw them leaving. He called his friend Benino at the hotel.

"I'll deal with them," said Benino.

He waited on the mountainside until Lady Penelope and Tin-Tin appeared. He was about to shoot when Parker grabbed him from behind. They tumbled down the slope together, rolling into a huge snowball, and crashed at the bottom. Benino was knocked out.

"He was sent to shoot you, m'lady," said Parker.

Back at the hotel, Tin-Tin showed Jeff a photograph of Mr Olsen's computer on the two-way TV.

"He's using a Cham-Cham," cried Brains. "Now I know how to change the message – by rewriting the music." He worked fast and sent the new music to Tin-Tin.

Tin-Tin rushed to give Cass the music, but Mr Olsen suddenly appeared. Tin-Tin hid. She saw Mr Olsen give Cass his own changes to the music.

"I'm sorry," said Cass when Mr Olsen had gone. "I have to do what he says."

The show started and the band began to play "Dangerous Game". "Only Penelope can save the transporter now," said Tin-Tin.

Lady Penelope walked on to the stage and started to sing. But she sang the tune that Brains had written and the band had to follow. Mr Olsen watched angrily.

Brains listened on the radio. "She's done it. She's changed the message!" he said.

Jeff turned to Virgil and Alan. "You'd better leave for Paradise Peaks Hotel right away," he said. "Penelope and Tin-Tin are in great danger."

Straight after the show, Lady Penelope, Tin-Tin and Parker made a quick getaway in a cable car. But Mr Olsen had followed them. He went to the cable-car control room and started destroying the controls. Suddenly, the cable car stopped.

Parker pressed the alarm button and Lady Penelope contacted Jeff. "Mr Olsen is after us," she said. "I thought we were getting away too easily."

"Keep calm," said Jeff. "Thunderbird 2 is on its way."

Meanwhile, Cass had heard the alarm ringing in the hotel and rushed out to investigate. He was amazed to see Mr Olsen in the control room, burning through the cable-car ropes. Cass grabbed him, but it was too late.

"You crazy fool," cried Cass. "The cables are free. That car will never stop. Everyone will be killed."

The cable car was now hurtling down the mountain out of control.

Suddenly Thunderbird 2 arrived and Alan started firing down ropes. Parker climbed on top of the cable car and caught them with his umbrella. He struggled to fasten the ropes to the car as it raced towards the ground.

He managed just in time and Thunderbird 2 pulled the cable car to a stop. Lady Penelope, Tin-Tin and Parker were saved.

The transporter had been saved too. Thanks to International Rescue, the enemy aircraft never received Mr Olsen's orders. The top-secret goods were delivered at last.

CARLTON
BOOKS

THIS IS A CARLTON BOOK

This edition first published in 2002 by Carlton Books Limited
An imprint of the Carlton Publishing Group
20 Mortimer Street
London W1T 3JW

First published by Carlton Books Limited as separate editions in 2000.

Text, illustrations and design © Carlton Books Limited 2000

™ and © 1965 and 1999. THUNDERBIRDS is a trademark of Carlton International Media Limited and is used under licence. THUNDERBIRDS is a Gerry Anderson Production. Licensed by Carlton International Media Limited.
© 1999. The CARLTON logotype device is a trademark of Carlton International Media Limited.

A CIP catalogue record for this book is available from the British Library.

ISBN 1 84222 732 7
Illustrations by County Studio
Language consultant Betty Root, formerly director of the Reading Centre, The University of Reading

Printed in Singapore

10 9 8 7 6 5 4 3 2 1